written & illustrated by Emma McCann

Emma McCann studied illustration at Kingston University. Her first picture book "Fish Don't Play Ball" was published by Meadowside Children's Books in June 2004. Her second, "Munch," followed in February 2005 and was long-listed for the Kate Greenway Medal.

supervised by WonKey LEE

Professor WonKey LEE has been teaching at Seoul National University of Education, and was President of the Korea Association of Primary English Education.

41 Bunny's T-shirt

Project Director Yeonhwan Park | **Publisher** Korea Hermannhesse Co., Ltd.
Editors Kkotnim Ku, Hyoyeong Kim, Yumi Kim | **Designers** Mikyong Park, Jaewook Kim, Jungah Park, Jiyoung Park | **Recording** EDGE Studio, New York
www.hermannhesse-book.co.kr

Korea Hermannhesse Co., Ltd.
444-148 Geumgok-dong Bundang-gu Seongnam-si
Gyeonggi-do Korea 463-480
Phone (031)715-7722 Fax (031)786-1100
7-3 Seokchon-dong Songpa-gu Seoul Korea 138-842
Phone (02)470-7722 Fax (02)470-8338

Sing Sing PHONICS Story Books

Bunny's T-shirt

written & illustrated by **Emma McCann**

Korea Hermannhesse

Tiger and **Bird** are at **home**.
They are painting *together*.

"I'm thirsty!" says Tiger.

7

Tiger goes to get **soda**.

Oh, no! **Tiger** trips!
The pot **bounces** and **bounces**.

9

Oh, no!
Bird is covered in paint!

10

Bird throws paint at **Tiger**!

11

Tiger and **Bird** are laughing.
They are covered in paint!

Bunny is **hurrying**
up the **hill**.

13

Bunny opens the door.

SPLAT!

14

"Oh, no! Paint is all over my **T-shirt!**"
Bunny howls.

15

Bunny sees paint everywhere!

There's even paint on **Tiger's teeth!**

Bunny begins to laugh.
"We're **sorry**," says **Tiger**.

18

"Never mind," says Bunny.
"I like this color better!"

19

Listen to the words and find the letters they start with.